The Baabaasheep Quartet

For black sheep everywhere — L.E.W.

In Canada
Fitzhenry & Whiteside Limited
195 Allstate Parkway
Markham, Ontario   L3R 4T8
www.fitzhenry.ca

In the United States
Fitzhenry & Whiteside Limited
121 Harvard Avenue, Suite 2
Allston, Massachusetts 02134
godwit@fitzhenry.ca

10 9 8 7 6 5 4 3 2 1

Library and Archives Canada Cataloguing in Publication

Watts, Leslie Elizabeth, 1961-
    The baabaasheep quartet / Leslie Elizabeth Watts.
ISBN 1-55041-890-4
1. Sheep—Juvenile fiction. I. Title.
PS8595.A8756B32 2005   jC813'.54   C2004-907278-1

**U.S. Publisher Cataloging-in-Publication Data
(Library of Congress Standards)**

Watts, Leslie Elizabeth, 1961-
    The baabaasheep quartet / Leslie Elizabeth Watts.
[32] p. : col. ill. ; cm.
Summary: After moving to the city, four sheep companions try in vain to find acceptance in the human world. But when they enter a barbershop quartet competition in the mistaken belief they'll be meeting other sheep, they discover that they don't have to blend in to belong.
ISBN 1-55041-890-4
1. Sheep — Fiction. I. Title.
[E] 22   PZ7.W388 2005

Fitzhenry & Whiteside acknowledges with thanks the Canada Council for the Arts, the Government of Canada through the Book Publishing Industry Development Program (BPIDP), and the Ontario Arts Council for their support of our publishing program.

Printed in Singapore
Design by Blair Kerrigan/Glyphics

The Baabaasheep Quartet

Leslie Elizabeth Watts

Fitzhenry & Whiteside

Once, four sheep retired from
the farm and went to live in the city.
For the first few weeks they were excited about their new life.
They decorated their apartment.

They ate in fancy restaurants. They attended the opera.

But try as they might, they did not quite fit in.

"There must be more to city life than this," Woolcott said over porridge one morning, and he sighed deeply.

"We need to find a way to belong," said Lambert.

Eugene tapped the table with his hoof. "We need a job," he said.

Waylon stopped humming into his orange juice. "But it has to be something we can do well."

They looked through the newspaper.

The four found a job with Lloyd's Lawn Care Company. Unfortunately, Woolcott clipped more than just the grass. "I'm sorry," said Lloyd at the end of the day, "but I won't be able to give you any work tomorrow."

Eugene suggested knitting sweaters for babies at the hospital.
Unfortunately, the hospital wasn't expecting any babies with four legs.
"I'm sorry," said the director, "but I don't think we can use those here."
"What about hats?" asked Lambert.
The director didn't think so.

Lambert thought they needed exercise.

They joined the Greenview Lawn Bowling League. Unfortunately, their hooves made a few holes in the lawn.

"I'm sorry," said the team manager, "but we won't be able to invite you back next week."

The four sheep walked home in the rain.
Waylon noticed a sign stapled to a lamppost.
He pulled it down and folded it carefully.

At dinner no one spoke. Just before
dessert, Waylon cleared his throat.
"I hope you don't mind," he said
rather nervously, "but I have an idea."
He brought out the sign and unfolded it.
Most of the words were still clear.

Eugene, Lambert, and Woolcott carefully read every word.

At last Eugene began to smile. "But, of course!" he cried. "A baabaasheep quartet! There are four of us and we are all sheep. Everyone knows that sheep sing beautifully."

Woolcott was delighted. "Why didn't we think of it before?"

Lambert clapped his hooves. "We'll have a chance to meet other sheep in the city. We'll be sure to fit in."

Waylon beamed. "Of course," he said, "we'll have to practice."

The friends practiced every day.
They sang in the shower and in
front of the sink.

They sang on the balcony.

They sang as they shopped.

They even placed a long distance call to their old friends on the farm.

On Saturday the four sheep took a taxi to the City Concert Hall.

"I don't see any other sheep," whispered Lambert.

"If we're the only contestants," Eugene told him, "then we'll definitely win."

"There certainly are a lot of people in striped jackets," said Woolcott.

"Let's not dilly-dally," said Waylon. "The contest starts in ten minutes."

As they entered the concert hall, Eugene stopped in his tracks.

Woolcott gulped.

Lambert gasped.

Waylon looked sheepish. "I guess I made a mistake," he said.

"No wonder there are no other sheep," said Eugene. "This is a contest for people who work in barbershops."

"People with moustaches," said Woolcott. "People who cut hair."

"We don't fit in here either," Lambert said miserably. "We'll have to go home."

"Wait," said Waylon. "I have an idea."

A few minutes later the Baabaasheep Quartet was on the stage. Although the four sheep were nervous, they sang beautifully and received a standing ovation. They sang three encores before they were declared the Grand Prizewinners.

Waylon was so happy that he wept, just a little. Unfortunately, his tears melted the glue that held his moustache in place. As the sheep mounted the stage to collect their award, the moustache slipped to the floor.

The audience fell silent.

For a moment Waylon
stood gazing at them. He was
petrified. He didn't know what to do.
Then he decided. He ran.
But before Waylon got far, one of
the judges called after him, "Excuse me,
Mr. Sheep! You've forgotten your prize."

Waylon stopped running and turned around. Everyone in the audience was smiling.

He was amazed. No one seemed to care that the four friends were sheep. No one minded that their moustaches were false, their hats were made of paper, and their stripes were painted with lipstick. The only thing that mattered was how well they sang.

Waylon was filled with joy. He made a little bow, and the audience clapped and cheered and stamped their feet.

From that day on, the Baabaasheep Quartet was a great success.
They were invited to tour the finest concert halls in the world.
They met many interesting people who were always glad to see them.

They never encountered any other singing sheep. But wherever they went, whenever they sang, they never again worried about fitting in.